THE FOURTH QUESTION

For my family and friends, who encouraged me to write
R.C.W.

For my mother
J.C.

Published by The Trumpet Club, Inc.,
a subsidiary of Bantam Doubleday Dell Publishing Group, Inc.,
1540 Broadway, New York, New York 10036.
"A Trumpet Club Special Edition" with the portrayal of a trumpet
and two circles is a registered trademark of
Bantam Doubleday Dell Publishing Group, Inc.

ISBN 0-440-84910-1

This edition published by arrangement with
Holiday House, Inc.

Printed in the United States of America
February 1996
1   3   5   7   9   10   8   6   4   2
UPR

THE FOURTH QUESTION

A CHINESE TALE

retold by

ROSALIND C. WANG

illustrated by

JU-HONG CHEN

A TRUMPET CLUB SPECIAL EDITION

Long, long ago, a young man named Yee-Lee and his mother lived by Lotus Lake, below Tien-Tai Mountain. When his mother became very, very old and could not work anymore, Yee-Lee rented another piece of land from the landlord and planted some rice and vegetables.

He worked very hard, night and day. But they never had enough food or clothing. Yee-Lee began to wonder, "Why, in spite of all my hard work, am I still so poor?"

One day, Yee-Lee heard that the Wise Man of Kun-lun
Mountain was very good at giving people advice to solve their
problems. He decided to go and seek advice from the Wise
Man.

Before he left, Yee-Lee stored rice, oil, salt, beans, and wood for his mother, enough to last for a long time. Then he started on his journey.

For forty-nine days, Yee-Lee walked and walked toward the west. Scorched with thirst, he knocked at a hut and asked for a drink. A kindly old woman invited him inside and gave him food and water. She asked him, "Why are you panting, young man? Where are you rushing to?"

"I am going to the palace at the top of Kun-lun Mountain," Yee-Lee replied, "to ask the Wise Man why I work so hard but am still poor."

When the old woman heard this, she grabbed his hands and pleaded, "Will you ask him something for me, too? I have a very beautiful and clever daughter who is eighteen years old. When she was born, I named her Ya-May, which means "graceful plum flower," but it also means "mute girl," because she has never spoken a word. Good young man, will you please ask the Wise Man why my daughter cannot speak?"

"I shall ask for you," promised Yee-Lee.

After spending the night in the old woman's hut, Yee-Lee continued his westward journey for another forty-nine days until he couldn't walk anymore. Then, he knocked at the door of a bamboo hut. An old man opened the door and invited him in. After serving him food and drink, the old man inquired, "Where are you going in such a hurry that you are sweating so much?"

"I am going to the palace at the top of Kun-lun Mountain to ask the Wise Man why I work so hard, but am still poor," answered Yee-Lee.

The old man's eyes became bright. He said with a laugh, "How lucky I am! I, too, have a problem. In my orchard is an orange tree with bushy green leaves, but it doesn't bear any fruit. Would you please find out what we can do about it?"

"I shall be glad to find out for you," Yee-Lee answered.

Early in the morning, as soon as the rooster crowed, Yee-Lee began his journey again. He came to a wide, wild river. There was neither ferry nor bridge to get across it. Yee-Lee sat down on a big rock by the riverbank and wondered how to cross. Suddenly, the river roared, the wind howled, and dark clouds covered the sun. Then, as the storm cleared, a rainbow appeared in the sky. A dragon emerged from the rushing river and called out, "Hey, young man, why do you sit there with such a sad face?"

Yee-Lee sighed and replied, "I am going to the palace on top of Kun-lun Mountain to ask the Wise Man why I work so hard and am still so poor. But now, with this big, wide river in front of me, and no ferry or bridge to take me across, I don't know what to do."

"I will carry you over!" said the dragon. "But you must promise to ask a question for me. I have hurt neither men nor animals in my life, and I have behaved myself for a thousand years. Why can't I rise to heaven?"

"I'll be sure to ask this question for you!" Yee-Lee quickly promised the dragon. In return, the dragon carried him across the river on his back.

After he had gone westward for another forty-nine days, Yee-Lee came to a gigantic, ancient city on top of the mountain. When he asked the guards where the Wise Man of Kun-lun lived, he was taken to a magnificent hall in the palace.

Sitting in the middle of this hall was an old man with silvery hair and a beard. Yee-Lee realized this must be the Wise Man of Kun-lun. Before he could utter a single word, the old man addressed him with a smile: "Why have you come here, young man?"

Yee-Lee bowed and replied politely, "Honorable Wise Man, my name is Yee-Lee. My mother and I live by Lotus Lake below Tien-Tai Mountain. I have come to seek your advice for four problems."

The Wise Man nodded his head and told him, "The rule here is to ask questions in odd numbers. Ask one question, but not two; ask three, but not four. Now you have four questions. Therefore, you can only ask three of them. Think it over and decide which one to leave out."

It was hard for Yee-Lee to decide. He thought about the questions over and over again. His own question was very important, but the three other questions were important, too. The images of the old woman, the old man, and the dragon flashed in front of his eyes again and again.

Since he was only allowed to ask three questions, he decided to give up his own and ask the others.

When the Wise Man had answered the three questions, Yee-Lee thanked him and went happily away from the palace of Kun-lun. When he came to the river, the dragon was waiting for him.

"Do you have an answer for me?" asked the dragon.

Yee-Lee said, "The Wise Man of Kun-lun told me that you must do two things before you can rise up to heaven."

"What are they? Please tell me quickly!" the dragon cried.

"First, you must carry me across the river. Second, you must remove the pearl which shines on your head at night."

The dragon agreed and gently carried the young man across the river. He then asked Yee-Lee to help him knock off the pearl. Immediately, two horns shot out from the dragon's head, and he rose toward the sky. When he pierced through the clouds, the dragon called down to Yee-Lee, "Thank you, my friend. Please keep the pearl as my gift to you. And remember, it is NOT an ordinary pearl."

Yee-Lee carefully wrapped the shining pearl in a handkerchief and continued on his journey home. When he arrived at the bamboo hut, the old man anxiously asked, "Did you do as you promised?"

"Yes I did," answered Yee-Lee. "The Wise Man of Kun-lun wanted me to tell you that twelve pots of gold and twelve pots of silver are buried at the bottom of the pool in your orchard. If you dig up the pots, and water the orange tree with water from the pool, the tree will produce sweet fruit."

The old man called his son to help. First, they scooped the
water out of the pool. Then they started to dig. Yee-Lee helped
them, too. They dug for several hours, but neither gold nor
silver appeared. They did not give up, however, but dug deeper
and deeper. Finally, they found twelve pots of gold and twelve
pots of silver. They took out the pots, and clear water sprang up
from the bottom of the pool and filled it up in a moment.

The old man watered the tree with the clear water as he had been advised. As soon as the water touched the roots, every branch of the tree bore fruit. Soon the whole tree was covered with oranges, the color of the sun. The old man was so thrilled that he asked Yee-Lee to stay a few more days. He also rewarded Yee-Lee with a pot of gold and a pot of silver. Nevertheless, Yee-Lee wanted to hurry home. He left the old man's house and carried with him the pearl that shone at night and the pots of gold and silver.

When he neared the old woman's hut, she ran out to meet him and inquired eagerly, "Have you done what I asked you to do?"

"Yes," he answered, "the Wise Man of Kun-lun wanted me to tell you that your daughter will be able to speak when she sees a man whom she loves."

Ya-May came in while her mother was talking to Yee-Lee. When the girl saw him, she blushed like a rose, smiled shyly, and asked, "Mother, who is this?"

The old woman was so happy that tears of joy rained down her cheeks like a waterfall.

She held Ya-May tightly in her arms and said, "This is a good sign, my child. Today you spoke your first words at the sight of this young man. He must be the one that heaven has arranged for you. Oh, praise the Wise Man of Kun-lun."

Yee-Lee was excited too, since he had fallen in love with the girl immediately. The whole village was filled with joy and happiness when they heard this good news. Everyone helped prepare for the wedding and showered the couple with food and gifts. Ya-May was no longer a mute girl, but a truly beautiful lady as graceful as a plum flower.

But Yee-Lee still worried about his mother. After his marriage, he bid farewell to the old woman and hurried toward his home with his pearl that shone at night, his pots of gold and silver, and his young bride.

When he arrived home, Yee-Lee found that his aged mother was now blind. She had cried and cried in fear that her son would never return. Yee-Lee wanted his mother to see his beautiful wife, but all she could do was feel Ya-May's smooth cheeks. He also wanted her to see the pots of gold and silver. But she could only hear the clinking sound of the precious metals. Finally, Yee-Lee took out the pearl and waved it before her eyes, but no matter how the pearl shone, all his mother could see was darkness.

Yee-Lee felt very sad and discouraged. He wished that his mother could see something, anything at all. And, as he wished, his mother's eyes became well again. She could see! How had this happened?

Suddenly Yee-Lee remembered what the dragon had said as he rose to heaven: "It is NOT an ordinary pearl." The pearl in his hands not only shone at night, but it granted his wish and helped his mother see again.

From that day on, Yee-Lee continued to work hard in the field. With Ya-May's help, they had enough food to eat and warm clothes to wear. Their life together was sweet and happy.

Although Yee-Lee had not asked the Wise Man of Kun-lun the fourth question, his own question, he found the answer to it anyway. Helping others and doing good deeds brought him happiness and rewards.